Boise State University Western Writers Series   Number 15

George Frederick Ruxton

By Neal Lambert

Brigham Young University

Editors: Wayne Chatterton
James H. Maguire

Business Manager:
James Hadden

Cover Illustration is a portion of "Bourgeois Walker and his Squaw," watercolor, Alfred Jacob Miller, from a sketch made in 1837. In *The West of Alfred Jacob Miller*, University of Oklahoma Press, 1950, p. 78. Courtesy of the Walters Art Gallery and the University of Oklahoma Press.

Cover Design by Arny Skov,
Copyright 1974

Boise State University, Boise, Idaho

Copyright 1974
by the
Boise State University Western Writers Series

ALL RIGHTS RESERVED

Library of Congress Card No. 74-1974

International Standard Book No. 0-88430-014-5

Printed in the United States of America by
The Caxton Printers, Ltd.
Caldwell, Idaho

WESTERN WRITERS SERIES

No. 15

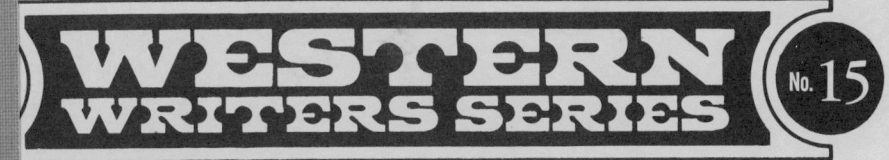

GEORGE FREDERICK RUXTON

by Neal Lambert

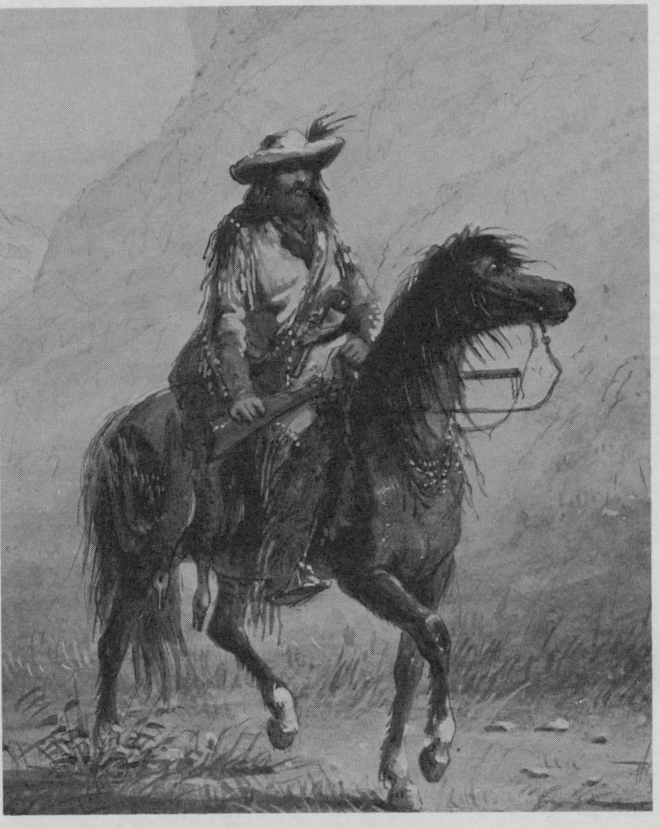

BOISE STATE UNIVERSITY
BOISE, IDAHO

George Frederick Ruxton

Soc
F
592
R8
L3

George Frederick Ruxton

In the spring of 1847 at Fort Leavenworth on the Indian frontier a group of United States Dragoons stood staring at a remarkable frontier figure with a "Mahogany-coloured face" and dressed in "the pride of fringed deerskin and porcupine quills." The costume was creating "no little difference of opinion amongst the troopers" as to which Indian tribe the figure might belong to.

"That's a Pottowatomie," said one, "by his red turban."

"How long have you been in the west," cried another, "not to know a Kickapoo when you see him?"

"Pshaw!" exclaimed a third; "that's a white trapper from the mountains. A regular mountain-boy that, I'll bet you a dollar."

One smart-looking dragoon, however, looked [closely at the] face, and, turning round to his comrades, said, "Well boys, I'll just bet you a dollar all round that that injun's no other than a British officer. Wagh! And what's more, I can tell you his name." (*Adventures in Mexico and the Rocky Mountains, 1846-1847*, p. 313)

This Indianized white man was, as the soldier recognized, George Frederick Ruxton, a British subject educated and trained in England, a former officer and veteran of a civil war and hand-to-hand combat, a traveler and adventurer with remarkable powers of survival and endurance, and a skillful writer from whose hand was to come one of the classics of Western American literature. If his dress was a symbol of his complete absorption into the life of the frontier, the notebooks in his saddle bags and the ideas in his head were evidence of his imaginative and artistic control of those experiences. His was one of those rare sensitivities which included not merely the ability to recall past experiences but, more importantly, the genius to shape those experiences in such a way that we can understand the significance of the experiences. We can understand their significance for the man who lived them as well as for ourselves. The power of this remarkable talent gives *Adventures in Mexico and the Rocky Mountains* and the more imaginative and now classic *Life in the Far West* their prominent positions on our present shelves of Western literature.

This leather-clad man at Fort Leavenworth, arranging for his travels back to his home in England, was born George Augustus Frederick Ruxton on July 24, 1821, in Oxfordshire, England. The third of six children, he could claim a rich heritage in Irish and Scottish ancestors and "plenty of soldiers and adventurers" on both sides of his progenitors (Voelker, "Ruxton of the Rocky Mountains," *Bulletin of the Missouri Historical Society*, January 1949, p. 79). When George was seven, his father moved the family to Broad Oak, an old rural estate about thirty miles southeast of London. But the father did not live to rear his son, whose school days were troublesome. As Ruxton tells us:

> Everything like restraint, and consequently all application to studies, was irksome to me, and but that I had fortunately a tolerable share of ability, a quick and ready talent, and a clear intellect which enabled me to seize at once upon ideas and adapt them to practical purposes, I should have entered the world totally uneducated. (Porter and Hafen, *Ruxton of the Rockies*, p. 3)

This wayward disposition finally led to Ruxton's expulsion from Sandhurst Military Academy, and by the time he was seventeen the young adventurer was making his way to Spain to join the loyalist army in that country's civil war. In the scraps of writing that record his impressions of the people he encountered, Ruxton demonstrates, even in the unfinished fragments of this experience, the eye and the ear, the special sensitivities which were to make the account of his travels on the American continent so significant for Western literature.

Ruxton was impressed by more than scenes of gross domestic life in the mountain borders of Spain. Though his record is brief, it is also clear and unflinching in its account of bloody battles, like the one in which an officer knocked the enemy from their horses, leaving them to be sabred by his men:

> cut and stab was the order of the day, and after showing fight for some time, the Factions fairly turned tail and ran for it, leaving three hundred on the field. No quarter was given or expected, and a scene of butchery commenced which defies description, and which our men could not be restrained in. (*Ruxton of the Rockies,* p. 31)

The young man who participated in such awesome slaughter was only seventeen when he returned to England.

After being decorated for his bravery in Spain, Ruxton came home, received his commission in the Ceylon Rifles, was transferred to the 89th Foot Regiment, and then was sent to Ontario, Canada.

His experience with the Canadian wilderness only enlarged his appetite for hunting and long travels through the woods. Having read and been inspired by the adventure and woodcraft in the novels of James Fenimore Cooper, he realized that he "had always longed to pull a trigger in the woods of America, and now the opportunity had arrived" (*Ruxton of the Rockies,*

p. 37). Breaking loose entirely from the army, Ruxton gave over his military career, sold his commission, hunted out his Indian friend Peshwego, and spent the winter of 1843-1844 as a *voyageur* in the frozen woods of Ontario and northern New York.

Ruxton returned to England in 1844, apparently with plans for new travels already forming in his mind. In June he set out for Northern Africa, but frustrated by the hostility of the people, he ended his expedition in the deserts and returned to England (*Ruxton of the Rockies,* p. 87). A few months later he was off again, this time to explore Southern Africa.

By now Ruxton's activities were attracting attention from important figures, and his trip to Africa was described at length in the 1845 anniversary speech of the President of the Royal Geographic Society (*Ruxton of the Rockies,* p. 88).

But impressive as the youth was, and as important as the scheme of exploring Southern Africa was, these plans, too, were frustrated. Ruxton almost lost his life depending on nonexistent rivers and uninhabited seaports. When the traders refused to co-operate, he had to abandon his African scheme, and disappointed for the second time, he returned to England. There he petitioned Her Majesty's Government for assistance, but even with the endorsement of the Royal Geographic Society the delays lengthened and multiplied. So when an opportunity for travel in North America presented itself, Ruxton started without delay on what was to become his Great Journey, an expedition that was to take him from the southern coasts of Mexico through the Rocky Mountains and the plains of the American West, a journey of over 2,000 miles. By the struggles and sufferings of his previous experience, he was well prepared for the enterprise.

For years a mystery surrounded Ruxton's motives for this endeavor. Some had suggested that the young traveler was a spy for the British government, gathering military information regarding the Mexican-American war. Ruxton himself was vague about the purposes of his trip: "It is hardly necessary to explain the cause of my visiting Mexico at such an unsettled period; and I fear that circumstances will prevent my gratifying the curiosity of the reader, should he feel any on that point" (*Adventures in Mexico and the Rocky Mountains, 1846-1847,* p. iii).

However, the likelihood of Ruxton's being a spy is rather small, for he was anything but covert in his movements and actions. A much better explanation of Ruxton's purposes is that offered by F. E. Voelker in his article on Ruxton. He brings together evidence which shows that Ruxton "was acting in the dual capacity of roving commercial attaché of the British diplomatic service and commercial agent of the Mexican government" ("Ruxton of the Rocky Mountains," p. 83). So Ruxton's ostensible purpose was to help re-establish the international trade along the Santa Fe trail which the war had temporarily interrupted. But he also had a much larger purpose which is for us more important: the compelling urge to test his idea of wilderness, and the opportunity to know firsthand the life of the American Far West. With these purposes driving him, Ruxton set out on his Great Journey.

Ruxton landed at Vera Cruz in August 1847, traveled northward through Mexico City, through Silao, Agua Caliente, Durango, Chihuahua, El Paso, Socorro, Santa Fe, Taos, past the Spanish Peaks, and down the front range of the Rockies to the Arkansas River and Pueblo. There he wintered with the old mountain man John Hawkens. He hunted, explored, and absorbed the stories, the legends, and the ways of the men of the early fur trade. Then he came back through St. Louis and went to England the following spring and summer.

All of this great journey was, as one can well imagine, filled with remarkable difficulties both human and Natural. Ruxton had to pass through whole towns of hostile Mexicans and through vast expanses of Indian territory where Apache war parties were roaming in search of easy scalps. He had to cross

9

parched deserts and snow-choked mountain passes. In Leon he was pursued by an angry band of Mexicans shouting, "Kill him, kill the Jackass," and Ruxton escaped only by stabbing one of the group to death (*Adventures,* pp. 68-69). He was thrown from his horse and kicked insensible, but afterward he rode forty-five miles in the sun, half unconscious and with a dislocated jaw (p. 78). His own servant tried to murder him, and thieves stole everything he had, though by torturing the culprits he was able to retrieve most of it (pp. 136-38). His horse dumped him into an ice-filled stream and rolled with him into a twenty-foot snow drift, severely injuring his ribs. Both of his hands and one foot were severely frostbitten, and he was given up for dead when he was trapped in prairie blizzards worse than "the 'oldest inhabitant' had ever witnessed" (p. 232). He missed being massacred at Arroyo Hondo by a matter of days and missed being burned alive in a mountain fire by a matter of minutes. That he was able to complete such a journey alive is in itself a feat almost incredible.

But, for us, the value of Ruxton's journey lies not so much in the accomplishment as in the impressions and materials that he brought back to England with him. For that reason, the most distressing occurrence of the whole trip may not have been so much the threatened loss of Ruxton's scalp as it was the actual loss of his papers as he made his way eastward toward civilization.

All that remained after water seeped into the pack containing his papers was a "rough notebook" and Ruxton's own recollections. This unfortunate experience may help explain Ruxton's next period of almost feverish writing.

With the long journey behind him and his head crammed with the stuff of the West, Ruxton returned to England and threw himself into a period of remarkable literary activity. Between August 1847 and June 1848, Ruxton finished a paper "On the Migration of the Ancient Mexicans, and their Analogy to the existing Indian Tribes of Northern Mexico." He wrote two sketches, "The Texan Ranger" and "The Battle of Buena Vista." And he prepared for publication the manuscripts for his two books, *Adventures in Mexico and the Rocky Mountains* and *Life in the Far West* ("Ruxton of the Rocky Mountains," pp. 87-88).

It was a striking burst of creative activity. By the end of December, *Adventures* was receiving enthusiastic compliments from reviewers, and Ruxton was being hailed as "Ruxton of the Rocky Mountains" (p. 88). By late spring of 1848 Ruxton's most ambitious work, *Life in the Far West,* was in the hands of the editors of *Blackwoods Edinburgh Magazine,* who were to publish the book serially beginning in June.

But by this time also, the vicissitudes of his strenuous life were having their effect on Ruxton. He had wrenched his back when he fell from a mule onto the stake of an Indian lodge in the Rockies, and the injury sometimes kept him bedfast, as he remarked in a letter to a friend: "I fear I injured my spine, for I have never felt altogether [well regarding] the thing since, and shortly after I saw you, the symptoms became rather ugly. However, I am now getting round again" (*Ruxton of the Rockies,* p. 308). All of this, however, did not keep Ruxton from dreaming of the mountains. Ill health notwithstanding, he exchanged his rights to *Life in the Far West* for some ready cash and set out again for America. In the lingo of the mountain men, he wrote his editors:

> As you say, human nature can't go on feeding on civilized fixings in this "big village"; and this child has felt like going West for many a month, being half froze for buffler meat and mountain doins. My route takes me *via* New York, the Lakes, and St. Louis, to Fort Leavenworth, or Independence on the Indian frontier. Thence packing my 'possibles' on a mule, and mounting a buffalo horse (Panchito, if he is alive), I strike the Santa Fe

trail to the Arkansas, away up that river to the mountains, winter in the Bayou Salade where Killbuck and La Bonté joined the Yutes, cross the mountains next spring to Great Salt Lake—and that's far enough to look forward to—always supposing my hair is not lifted by Comanche or Pawnee on the scalping route of the Coon Creeks and Pawnee Fork. (*Life in the Far West,* pp. xiii-xiv)

Ruxton visited his brother in Halifax, Nova Scotia; and at Buffalo, on his way to St. Louis, he met Lewis H. Garrard who was soon to begin work on his own *Wah-to-yah and the Taos Trail.* Garrard and Ruxton talked about familiar places and people of the West and about *Life in the Far West,* which was by then well into its serial publication. Ruxton went on to St. Louis, but his health deteriorated even more; and contracting dysentery he died there on August 29, 1848.

He had earned the Cross of San Fernando with the title of Knight in the Spanish Civil War. He had been an army officer in Ireland and Canada. He had tramped and hunted in the Woods of Canada and New York, experienced desert life in Morocco, and explored in South Africa. He had traveled 2,000 miles—much of it alone— through hostile country where his own life was in constant jeopardy. He had written two influential books, one of which was to become a classic in the literature of the West. When he was buried in the old Christ Church Cemetery in St. Louis, he had just celebrated his twenty-seventh birthday ("Ruxton of the Rocky Mountains," p. 89).

When George Ruxton sat down with his rough notebook to begin work on *Adventures in Mexico . . . ,* he had no intention of writing what we usually think of as a piece of "literature." Indeed, he was self-conscious about this book that he referred to as his "little work," apologizing that the loss of his detailed notes made possible only "a brief outline of the journey." He preferred this brevity, he said, to using "the treacherous note-book of memory, or the less reliable source of a fertile imagination" (*Adventures,* p. iii). So he wrote the account of his remarkable journey through the North American frontier, Ruxton had by his own statement "no higher aim than to give an idea of the difficulties and hardships a traveler may anticipate, should he venture to pass through it and mix with its semi-barbarous and uncouth people, and to draw a faint picture of the lives of those hardy pioneers of civilization whose lot is cast upon the boundless prairies and rugged mountains of the Far West" (p. iii).

Ruxton's modest declaration is a poor indication of both the significance and the complexity of his remarkable work. For while Ruxton may make every effort to present merely the outline of his travels, one is conscious over and over again of the presence of this man, not merely as traveler, or even as adventurer, but as an artist, as a man sensitive to the higher meanings behind the things he saw and heard and experienced.

Ruxton's modesty does not diminish the effect of the day-to-day narrative itself. For as Ruxton moves up the continent one becomes gradually aware of the incremental power of an almost daily record of events. One becomes aware, for instance, of a slow change not only in the configuration of the landscape, but in the image of the Mexicans themselves. There is, on Ruxton's part, a slow accretion of distaste and finally of disgust as the people he meets have fewer and fewer of the qualities he admires. Thus the images he uses in describing the people become more and more those of animals and the lower forms of life. In the descriptions of the native inhabitants of Mexico City which we get early in the book, Ruxton is almost one with the natives, intense and interested, a sympathetic observer of the fandangos and knife fights (pp. 39-48). But by the time Ruxton has traveled into the northern country of New Mexico, his disgust is full and, both as traveler and as narrator, he holds himself aloof from his subject:

> No state of society can be more wretched or degrading than the social and moral condition of the inhabitants of New Mexico: but in this remote settlement, anything I had formerly imagined to be the *ne plus ultra* of misery, fell far short of the reality:—such is the degradation of the people of the Rio Colorado. Growing a bare sufficiency for their own support, they hold the little land they cultivate, and their wretched hovels, on sufferance from the barbarous Yutas, who actually tolerate their presence in their country for the sole purpose of having at their command a stock of grain and a herd of mules and horses, which they make no scruple of helping themselves to, whenever they require a remount or a supply of farinaceous food. (pp. 208-09)

The Mexicans are now reduced to the insignificance of penned animals. One is not surprised to read that when Ruxton crossed the border he looked back at the adobes of the last Mexican village, and "without one regret cried 'Adios, Mejico!' " (p. 210).

But this growing antipathy towards Mexico is only one of the elements which draw the reader on through the book, for if we are caught up by Ruxton's descriptions of the Mexicans in general, we are even more fascinated by the striking series of particular characters that Ruxton portrays for us with all the vigor and freshness of immediate experience. He says of the famous General Don Antonio Lopez de Santa Anna:

> His countenance completely betrays his character: indeed, I never saw a physiognomy in which the evil passions, which he notoriously possesses, were more strongly marked. Oily duplicity, treachery, avarice, and sensuality are depicted in every feature, and his well-known character bears out the truth of the impress his vices have stamped upon his face. (p. 18)

Besides such famous Mexicans as the General, Ruxton presents us with many obscure people, remarkable in their own right, who are rendered with an even more striking vividness and with bolder strokes. Ruxton's host at the little village of Temascateo is one of many such portraits:

> Fat and pulque lined, his heavy head, with large fishy eyes, almost sank into his body, his neck, albeit of stout proportion, being inadequate to support its enormous burden. Concealed from his sight behind the sensible horizon of a capacious paunch, a pair of short and elephantine legs shook beneath their load. The stolid heavy look of this mountain of meat was inexpressible. (p. 63)

The slight hyperbole of this passage is carefully and delicately managed. We see not only a very fat man, but also a brilliant authorial performance as Ruxton creates heavy rhythms and expanding, alliterative polysyllables to match his fleshy subject.

Not all the memorable characters of *Adventures* are people. It is difficult, for instance, to forget the "sullen and cowardly" coyote that Ruxton chases across the prairie (p. 160), or his "family" of horses and mules, or the pathetic prairie dog, "roused from his warm bed, and almost congealed with terror, by hearing the snorting yelp of the half-famished wolf, who, . . . with almost superlupine strength, hurls down the well-cemented walls, tears up the passages, lunges his cold nose into the very chambers, snorting into them with his earth-filled nose, in ravenous anxiety, and drives the poor little trembling inmate into the most remote corners, too often to be dragged forth, and unhesitatingly devoured" (pp. 298-99).

For many readers, the most significant figures of *Adventures* are the mountain men who either in person or as characters in brief narratives move through the last half of the book. Rube Thatcher, John Hawkens, William Bent, Bill Williams, Markhead, Harwood, and even **Hugh Glass** are only some of the men of the fur trade, famous and obscure, whom Ruxton mentions. Markhead, for instance, is characterized as a man celebrated "for his courage and reckless daring." While traveling with Sir William Drummond Stewart, Markhead overhears the Scottish hunter say in annoyed vexation that he would give five hundred dollars for the scalp of the thief. "The next day Markhead rode into camp with the scalp of the unfortunate horse-thief hanging at the end of his rifle, and I believe received the reward, at least so he himself declared to me, for this act of the mountain law" (p. 233).

Ruxton tells at some length, and with considerable vividness and power, the story of **Hugh Glass** (John Glass as Ruxton calls him) and his wrestle with the grizzly:

> The hunter, notwithstanding his hopeless situation, struggled manfully, drawing his knife and plunging it several times into the body of the beast, which, furious with pain, tore with tooth and claw the body of the wretched victim, actually baring the ribs of flesh, and exposing the very bones. Weak with loss of blood, and with eyes blinded with the blood which streamed from his lacerated scalp, the knife at length fell from his hand, and Glass sank down insensible, and to all appearance dead. . . . Poor Glass presented a horrifying spectacle: the flesh was torn in strips from his chest and limbs, and large flaps strewed the ground; his scalp hung bleeding over his face, which was also lacerated in a shocking manner. (p. 271)

Though Ruxton's account is different in some respects from other accounts, the bloody details of the struggle with the bear, the subsequent crawl back to the outpost, and the reunion with the trappers make up one of the important contributions to the Glass cycle.

The skill with which Ruxton creates these character sketches is part of the same talent that makes so memorable the incidents in which these people appear. Ruxton was an uncommon raconteur. Almost every phase of his journey is punctuated by tales, anecdotes, and legends told with a keen sense of detail and a good sense of pace and climax. Ruxton could turn the breaking of a dinner pot into a kind of mock-epic calamity (p. 163), and he could sustain a quiet note of domestic pathos as he recounted the story of a family destroyed spiritually by Indian attacks and paternal cowardice (pp. 82-83). His treatment of the Indian legend of the "Medicine" springs is as straightforward and as unquestioning as though an Indian were explaining the origin of the sacred mineral waters (pp. 253-57), and in his account of the massacre at Turley's mill (pp. 234-38), Ruxton is able with great skill to step back as a personality, moving out of the narrative, thus leaving the reader with little or no sense of authorial presence and in direct contact with the events themselves. Still, however interesting they may be, these narratives are, in the number of pages they cover, subordinate elements of the book.

At least as interesting to many readers is Ruxton's inclusive detail of the means and materials of mountain life. The animals and their habits, the methods of trapping and skinning, the tools, and the techniques of survival appear in such richness that if pulled together in one place they might well serve as a handbook for the fur trade. For instance, Ruxton discusses the grizzly bear and its habits, big horn sheep, elk, antelope, mountain wolves, buffalo, and, of course, beaver—giving a technical description of how to look for sign, how to prepare and bait the trap, and how to skin the animal and prepare the fur.

Ruxton also pays particular attention to the rendezvous, drawing in detail the scenes of this aspect of mountain life:

> The rendezvous is one continued scene of drunkenness, gambling, and brawling and fighting, as long as the money and credit of the trappers last. Seated, Indian

fashion, around the fires, with a blanket spread before them, groups are seen with their "decks" of cards, playing at "euker," "poker," and "seven-up," the regular mountain games. The stakes are "beaver," which here is current coin; and when the fur is gone, their horses, mules, rifles, and shirts, hunting-packs, and *breeches,* are staked. . . . There goes "hos and beaver!" is the mountain expression when any great loss is sustained; and, sooner or later, "hos and beaver" invariably find their way into the insatiable pockets of the traders. (pp. 245-46)

This combined vividness and concreteness of detail explains why many readers find this book such a rich source of factual material.

But as important as the details, the characters, and the narratives may be, they are not really the center of this book. The character of Ruxton himself gives the work its unity and wholeness. A recitation of this man's experiences makes a narrative as compelling in itself as any he may have heard around the campfires of his journey. We have already mentioned his being attacked by a band of Mexican killers, knives in hand, rushing at him in the darkness of a dead end street. As the first one ran at him, he stepped quickly to one side and at the same time made a stab with his own knife. The man, stumbling on forward, went to his knees crying, "*Dios! me ha matado.*" The second one ran to help the dying attacker while the last Mexican turned towards Ruxton. Seeing the Englishman with his knife ready and still willing to defend himself, he hesitated, allowing Ruxton to escape (p. 69). Farther North and later in the winter, Ruxton was trying to force his way through the snow-choked ridges of the Sangre de Cristo mountains when he was caught in a January blizzard. While trying to descend to the protection of the lower plains, the horses, mules, and men tumbled over the edge of a plateau, landing in a twelve-foot snow drift. Before an animal could move, every pack had to be removed, with the temperature ten degrees below zero and a hurricane-force wind driving the snow and cold against them. Finding further descent impossible, they had to make their way back up an almost perpendicular slope through six feet of snow. Ruxton had to beat a way for the lunging animals by throwing himself bodily into the snow and pounding it down. When a large grouse flew up, he tried to shoot it but could not cock his gun. His hands were useless from the cold. Nearly frozen, with darkness coming on, and still lost in the tops of the mountains, Ruxton observed that their situation was "anything but pleasant" (p. 219). Watching Ruxton encounter and survive so many dangers is enough to hold almost any reader close to the pages of *Adventures in Mexico and the Rocky Mountains.*

To the serious reader, this book also offers more complex concerns. For Ruxton reveals himself as a complex human being, a man who combines a degree of aristocratic and perhaps even racial pride with a genuine fondness for the savage, unstructured life of the frontier. That Ruxton had adopted many of the outward ways of the frontier is obvious from his dress, his equipment, and his skill with a gun. But it may well be that he had absorbed many of the inner values as well. For instance, camped by some mineral springs, Ruxton writes, "After my frugal breakfast, unseasoned by bread or salt, or by any other beverage than the refreshing soda-water, I took my rifle and sallied up to hunt, consigning my faithful animals to the protection of the Dryad of the fountain, offering to that potent sprite the never-failing 'medicine' of the first whiff of my pipe before starting from the spot" (p. 259). This and other such accounts of Ruxton's indulgence in Indian "medicine" are not condescending jests. Though some of the formal vocabulary suggests that the author maintains a distance between himself and his material, the account itself suggests that Ruxton was more than half-serious about such observances. He may have become more Indianized than he cared to admit. This sense of a deeper commitment assures us all the more of the validity of Ruxton's insights. He was not simply writing out of an inkpot, manufacturing images in the current literary fashion. He was instead working from a deep level of his own experience.

But in spite of the democratization that goes with such an immersion in the Western experience, Ruxton never relinquished his claim as an Englishman to a kind of cultural superiority. Over the Mexicans his superiority was grand. In his relationships with the Americans, there seemed more subtle differences, but the differences are a part of the book, nevertheless. Ruxton felt that the American army was remarkably undisciplined, that American manners were often laughable, and that slavery was a great blot on the country.

There is, too, a rather proud detachment in Ruxton's depiction of his own abilities and his self-confidence as a frontiersman. This tone is particularly strong in his description of his solitary mountain camp in the midst of hostile Indian country: "At night I returned to camp, made a fire, and cooked an appola of antelope meat, and enjoyed my solitary pipe after supper with as much relish as if I was in a divan, and lay down on my blanket, serenaded by packs of hungry wolves, and sleeping as soundly as if there were no such people in existence as Arapahoes, merely waking now and then and raising my hand to the top of my head, to assure myself that my top-knot was in its place" (p. 250).

To many readers, however, such an attitude is more pleasing than otherwise, for it is not empty pride. It is rather an assurance based on an earned self-confidence—on a self-reliance and independence which is not merely physical but philosophical. A good example of the effects of his attitude is Ruxton's response to his servant's attempt to shoot him in the back and steal his goods while they are alone on the trail. He writes, "I halted and took from him everything in the shape of offensive weapon, not excepting his knife; and wound up a sermon, which I deemed it necessary to give him, by administering a couple of dozen—well laid on with the buckle-end of my surcingle, at the same time giving him to understand, that if, hereafter, I had reason to suspect that he had even dreamed of another attempt upon my life, I would pistol him without a moment's hesitation. —Distance from El Chorro thirty-six miles" (p. 109). This is a strange passage, particularly in the detached, matter-of-fact tone. Moreover, the juxtaposition of details is startling—a sermon which ends with a vicious lashing and a threat of death, set next to a mundane record of miles traveled. These details do not hold to the generally accepted values of comparative and climactic order.

Ruxton may simply have been so amused at the inept attempt on his life that he could not become serious in writing about the matter, or he may not have been particularly concerned about death. Yet the tone of this passage is that of a man keenly aware of the imminent and daily possibility of violent death with which he must live. At the same time, he seems to be a man who refuses to be overwhelmed by such an awareness, a man who recognizes, even in such situations, his own ability to choose and to act. This is a tough-minded world view in which values and meanings derive from what our age would call the man's existential view of himself.

To talk of Ruxton as a potential prototype for significant Western fiction is to find ourselves some distance away from Ruxton's stated purpose for *Adventures*. Yet the unconscious genius of the writing is evidence that we are within the literary bounds of the book. It is obvious by now that "the treacherous notebook of memory" and the "less reliable source of a fertile imagination" were neither treacherous nor unreliable but were appropriate and significant wellsprings for the "little" travel book that Ruxton produced.

If *Adventures* transcends its stated purpose, it points the way to *Life in the Far West,* which was soon to be written. For in *Adventures* the literary artist is at work. There is evidence of conscious composition in some of Ruxton's descriptive passages. He had an experienced painter's eye and was a competent judge of art (p. 37). So, not surprisingly, his landscapes are often rendered in the unmistakable fashion of the painter. In describing the sunset over Jarral Grande, a village destroyed by Indians, Ruxton writes, "In the distance, the ragged outline of the sierra was golden with its declining rays, which shed a soft light on the ruins of the village; and everything looked so calm and beautiful, that it was difficult to call to mind that this was once the scene of horrid barbarities" (p. 128).

And in describing the sunrise from the base of Pike's Peak, he creates this vivid scene:

> While the deep gorge in which I lay was still buried in perfect gloom, the mountain-tops loomed grey and indistinct from out the morning mist. A faint glow of light broke over the ridge which shut out the valley from the east, and, spreading over the sky, first displayed the snow-covered peak, a wreath of vapoury mist encircling it, which gradually rose and disappeared. Suddenly the dull white of its summit glowed with light like burnished silver; and at the same moment the whole eastern sky blazed, as it were, in gold, and ridge and peak, catching the refulgence, glittered with the beams of the rising sun, which at length, peeping over the crest, flooded at once the valley with its dazzling light. (p. 259)

In these passages the gloom and bright light, the ruins and mists are an important quality of much early nineteenth-century landscape painting.

But those painters were working out of their own firsthand

experiences with nature, and it would be a mistake to think that Ruxton's response to the wilderness was entirely formal. It would be more accurate to say that he saw scenes which corresponded well with the picturesque, the beautiful, and the sublime that he was familiar with in the visual arts.

Ruxton made constant use of all his senses to discover, to remember, and to record the truths of his experience. So that even while writing this ostensibly objective account, he goes to considerable lengths to render with variety and artistic skill not only the things he saw, but the things he heard as well. He presents us with a striking gallery of living figures whose vernacular speech becomes a true feat of imaginative recreation. Ruxton is, perhaps, more famous for this feat of the imagination than for anything else, and rightly so.

He recreates, for instance, the mountain speech of two exuberant young teamsters as they approach the edges of civilization:

> "Wagh!" exclaimed one raw-boned young giant, as a bee flew past; "this feels like the old 'ooman, and mush and molasses at that! if it don't, I'll be doggone!"
>
> "Horroo for old Missouri!" roared another; "h'yar's a hos as will knock the hind sights off the corn-doins. Darn my old heart if that arn't a reg'lar-built hickory—makes my eyes sweat to look at it! This child will have no more 'mountains' horroo for old Missouri! Wagh!" (pp. 308-09)

This is the kind of speech which has made Ruxton famous. But there are differences in rhythm, syntax, and vocabulary which separate the next two speeches from each other and from the speech just above. The first is by a half-demented soldier just rescued from dying of thirst in the desert:

> "Stranger," he said to me, "you have been about the world, I guess, and are likely to know. What," he asked,

putting his face close to mine, "might be the worth in your country of a camlet cloak? I never see sech a cloak as that ar one in no parts," he continued, looking up into the sky as if the spectre of the camlet cloak was there. (p. 132)

By contrast, the following speech is from an old Yankee wagon driver:

> Cuss sich a darned country, I say! Wall, strangers, an ugly camp this, I swar; and what my cattle ull do I don't know, for they have not eat since we put out of Santa Fé, and are darned near giv out, that's a fact; and thar's nothin' here for 'em to eat, surely. Wall, they must just hold on till to-morrow, for I have only got a pint of corn apiece for 'em to-night anyhow, so there's no two ways about that. (pp. 187-88)

Such variety and explicitness in speech patterns represents for Ruxton a fortunate combination of a keenly sensitive ear and a true artistic ability to recreate. Especially in the last two examples, the language itself provides a glimpse into the mind of each speaker and into the narrow, discontinuous, yet entirely different worlds that each inhabits. It is at once amusing and pathetic.

Holding himself so close to his own sensory experience was a demanding task for a relatively inexperienced writer such as Ruxton. Sorting out and arranging the myriad details of such experiences would have been too demanding for a lesser talent. That Ruxton succeeded as well as he did is a tribute to his genius. But one of the real difficulties is that sometime in the process the writer has to ask himself about the meanings of those observations and the feelings they elicit. In writing about the life of the mountain man, Ruxton was confronted by some profound questions about the mature man and his place in the natural world. On the one hand the mountain man represented to Ruxton a distinct example of a lower form of human life; if not an animal, the mountain man was at least a distant primitive, standing far down the scale of civilized development:

> Knowing no wants save those of nature, their sole care is to procure sufficient food to support life, and the necessary clothing to protect them from the rigorous climate. This with the assistance of their trusty rifles, they are generally able to effect, but sometimes at the expense of great peril and hardship. . . . Their animal qualities, however, are undeniable. Strong, active, hardy as bears, daring, expert in the use of their weapons, they are just what uncivilized white man might be supposed to be in a brute state, depending upon his instinct for the support of life. (pp. 241-42)

With that same insight came a view of the natural world that no English moor could ever have revealed. On more than one occasion Ruxton found himself coping with a wilderness that was not only beyond domestication but even beyond description in any terms which made it meaningful for man: "The perfect solitude of this vast wilderness was almost appalling. From my position on the summit of the dividing ridge I had a bird's eye view, as it were, over the rugged and chaotic masses of the stupendous chain of the Rocky Mountains, and the vast deserts which stretched away from their eastern bases; while, on all sides of me, broken ridges, and chasms and ravines, with masses of piled-up rocks and uprooted trees, with clouds of drifting snow flying through the air, and the hurricane's roar battling through the forest at my feet, added to the wildness of the scene, which was unrelieved by the slightest vestige of animal or human life" (p. 218).

Certainly such a natural world takes little or no account of the human efforts which Ruxton represents. This was not, in any sense of the word, a man-centered world. And the age-old question—what is man?—took on a new and terrifying dimension. For, at least in one sense, the answer was—nothing. The Western mountains and the men who lived in them were profound experiences for Ruxton. He saw with his eyes and felt in his bones a world that denied for man the assumptions about his importance and his nobility which give meaning and significance to his efforts.

On the other hand, Ruxton did not flee with civilized horror from this natural world and its disturbing implications. As he tells us near the end of his mountain experience:

> When I turned my horse's head from Pike's Peak I quite regretted the abandonment of my mountain life, solitary as it was, and more than once thought of again taking the trail to the Bayou Salado, where I had enjoyed such good sport.
>
> Apart from the feeling of loneliness which any one in my situation must naturally have experienced, surrounded by stupendous works of nature, which in all their solitary grandeur frowned upon me, and sinking into utter insignificance the miserable mortal who crept beneath their shadow; still there was something inexpressibly exhilarating in the sensation of positive freedom from all worldy care, and a consequent expansion of the sinews, as it were, of mind and body, which made me feel elastic as a ball of Indian rubber, and in a state of perfect *insouciance*. (p. 280)

If in writing *Adventures* Ruxton uncovered profound and complex issues regarding the nature of man and the value of the wilderness, he also recognized that the format of a travel narrative has certain restrictions and difficulties. What Ruxton needed now was a format less tied to the events of his own journey, one which would give greater range to the artistic abilities he had already discovered in himself, one which would provide the probing imagination freedom to recreate and to form more fully the dramatic patterns suggested by the life of the frontiersman of the mountain West.

After finishing the manuscript of *Adventures in Mexico and the Rocky Mountains,* therefore, Ruxton turned his attention to a more consciously imaginative book, a work that was to become a classic of Western American literature, *Life in the Far West. Life* is an episodic narrative that follows the experiences of two mountain men, Killbuck and La Bonté. The first is older, a thorough-going mountain man who has been everywhere in the mountains and has seen everything. The latter man is younger but no less a mountain man. Having killed a rival in a duel over the love of Mary Brand, La Bonté has fled to the West, avoiding the penalties of civilized law but having to leave his Kentucky sweetheart. The novel opens with an Indian raid on the trappers' camp. There is a chase and a counterattack in which the two trappers succeed in recovering their stolen horses and mules and in lifting "Rapaho" hair. After the heroes have wintered with the friendly Yutahs, they meet a younger hunter (Ruxton himself), and around a blissful campfire they recount their wanderings and exploits, particularly the career of La Bonté. At this point, Ruxton says, "Perhaps it will be as well, to render La Bonté's mountain language intelligible, to translate it at once to tolerable English, and tell in the third person, but from his lips, the scrapes which him befell in a sojourn of more than twenty years in the Far West, and the causes which impelled him to quit the comfort and civilisation of his home, and seek the perilous but engaging life of a trapper in the Rocky Mountains" (*Life,* p. 58).

These episodes from La Bonté's career make up the main sections of the book. Ruxton follows this career through twenty years of mountain life: the difficulties in Kentucky; the arrival in St. Louis and the West; the transformation from greenhorn to mountain man; the struggles with Indians, cold, hunger; the adventures of a California horse-stealing expedition; and the rough delights of a Taos fandango. After recounting these adventures, Ruxton comes back to the trio around the campfire, where the subject of the Mormon migration comes up. In this context we learn that the Brands are traveling west with a group of Mormons and have recently struck out on their own through hostile Indian territory.

Thus the stage is set for the expected final scene, which is played true to form, with the three men rushing to a last-minute rescue of the Brand wagons and with Mary fainting appropriately into the arms of her La Bonté. As the story ends, La Bonté turns east with the Brand family wagons and his bride-to-be, and old Killbuck turns west with his grizzled mule, "pursuing his solitary way." Such is the bare outline of the plot of *Life in the Far West,* but as with *Adventures,* that outline gives no indication of the true significance of the book.

No longer limited to his own point of view, Ruxton could by virtue of his own imagination transform himself into an active participant in episodes and events about which he had only heard. By combining his own experience with the stories of his campfire colleagues in the crucible of his imagination, he was able to formulate and color important patterns of experience in the life of the mountain man in a way that has won the admiration of a wide range of readers.

Some writers and scholars of the Western experience have a special fondness for *Life in the Far West* because of the rich fund of "authentic" materials which it contains. As Bruce Sutherland says of Ruxton:

> The chief greatness of his achievement, however, lies in the fact that he preserved the stories told him by his mountain friends in much the same form that he first heard them. Personalities too are revealed, the men

who told the stories and the chief actors in the events described are portrayed . . . as individual human beings. ("George Frederick Ruxton in North America," *Southwest Review* [1944], p. 90)

LeRoy R. Hafen, one of the foremost historians of the mountain man, speaks of *Life* as "fictionalized history," reminding us that Ruxton's firsthand experience makes the book what it is: "Having roasted buffalo humps and rolled in a blanket before a trapper campfire, Ruxton . . . could describe the fascinating life of fur men and express their thoughts in their own distinctive jargon" (Hafen, ed., *Life in the Far West* [1951], p. xiii).

When *Life* was first published, the editors advised that it was to be read as "pictures from life, the results of the author's experiences," a view which Ruxton himself seemed to encourage when he wrote his editors, "There is no incident in it which has not actually occurred, nor one character who is not well known in the Rocky Mountains, with the exception of two whose names are changed—the originals of these being, however, equally well known with the others" (*Life,* p. 232). So *Life* has become an excellent source book for the life and times of the mountain man, exceeding in clarity and brilliance even the details given in *Adventures.* For in this account the writer's imagination was free to add sights, sounds, and smells in a way that was previously impossible. He felt free to give complete and meticulous attention to the details of Old Bill Williams' costume and accouterments:

> His buckskin hunting-shirt, bedaubed until it had the appearance of polished leather, hung in folds over his bony carcass; his nether extremities being clothed in pantaloons of the same material (with scattered fringes down the outside of the leg—which ornaments, however, had been pretty well thinned to supply "whangs" for mending moccasins or pack-saddles), which, shrunk

with wet, clung tightly to his long, spare, sinewy legs. His feet were thrust into a pair of Mexican stirrups, made of wood, and as big as coal-scuttles; and iron spurs of incredible proportions, with tinkling drops attached to the rowels, were fastened to his heel—a bead-worked strap, four inches broad, securing them over the instep. In the shoulder-belt which sustained his powder-horn and bullet-pouch, were fastened the various instruments essential to one pursuing his mode of life. An awl, with deer-horn handle, and the point defended by a case of cherry-wood carved by his own hand, hung at the back of the belt, side by side with a worm for cleaning the rifle; and under this was a squat and quaint-looking bullet mould, the handles guarded by strips of buckskin to save his fingers from burning when running balls, having for its companion a little bottle made from the point of an antelope's horn, scraped transparent, which contained the "medicine" used in baiting the traps. (pp. 112-13)

In their detail of mountain dress the paintings of Alfred Jacob Miller are no more complete and authentic than this passage. Not only do we have a list of the tools that a mountain man might carry, but we have in this description a sense of the physical reality of these particular tools: the cherry wood awl case and the buckskin covered handles of the bullet mold, even to the beaded spur strap "four inches broad."

He is equally vivid in capturing the details of a mountain camp as a rainstorm begins: "Huge drops of rain fell at intervals, hissing as they fell on the blazing fires, and pattered on the skins which the hunters were hurriedly laying on their exposed baggage. The mules near the camp cropped the grass with quick and greedy bites round the circuit of their pickets, as if conscious that the storm would soon prevent their feeding, and were already humping their backs as the chilling rain fell upon their flanks" (p. 16). There is immediacy and rightness to the mules' "quick and greedy bites" and their humped backs. This remarkable particularity, coupled with Ruxton's virtuosity in recording mountain man speech, is the main reason why historians and imaginative writers have considered *Life* such an important supply of firsthand information.

The significance of *Life* as an influence upon the imaginative literature of the fur trade can hardly be exaggerated. Almost every mountain man novel has borrowed directly or indirectly bits and snatches or even whole episodes from Ruxton's earlier classic. In his novel *Mountain Man,* Vardis Fisher uses Ruxton's story of a game of hands played between a Burntwood Sioux and a Crow warrior. As the game progresses, the Sioux loses more and more, and at last bets his scalp. After winning the scalp, too, the Crow agrees to meet his gore-covered opponent later at the same spot to continue the game. When they meet for the second time, luck has changed sides, and the Crow loses all—even his own scalp. Betting his life against the other's winnings, the Crow loses for the last time, and the victorious Sioux "plunged his knife into his heart to the very hilt." The same story, slightly expanded in detail, is an interesting set piece in Fisher's book *(Mountain Man,* pp. 175-76).

Ruxton's account of the Taos fandango, where the rough mountain men riot in the Mexican dance halls and steal the Taos beauties, is the basis for a central episode in Harvey Fergusson's *Wolf Song.* This borrowing is striking in at least one detail: in Ruxton's account, La Bonté is attracted to the Mexican Dolores Salazar; in Fergusson's account, Sam Lash falls in love with Lola Salazar *(Wolf Song,* pp. 79-86). Similar fandangos appear in Stewart Edward White's *The Long Rifle* and Mayne Reid's *The Scalp Hunters;* and Lewis H. Garrard includes such an interlude in his *Wah-to-yah and the Taos Trail.*

Many novelists have borrowed directly from the language of

Ruxton's pages. Such phrases as "half froze," "this child," "this nigger," "rubbed out," "don't shine," and the bear-like "wagh" have become so familiar that readers may not realize that Ruxton is our main source for this language. Ruxton's retelling of Black Harris's visit to the "putrefied" forest is followed very closely by Fergusson as he puts the same story into the mouth of Rube Thatcher in *Wolf Song*. And one famous passage has been lifted out of *Life* almost verbatim not once but twice. In Ruxton's account, La Bonté and Killbuck are snow-bound and starving. Killbuck, weakened further by an old wound, calls his friend to his side:

> "Boy," he said, "this old hos feels like goin' under, and that afore long. You're stout yet, and if thar was meat handy, you'd come round slick. Now, boy, I'll be under, as I said, afore many hours, and if you don't raise meat you'll be in the same fix. I never eat dead meat myself, and wouldn't ask no one to do it neither; but meat fair killed is meat any way; so, boy, put your knife in this old niggur's lights, and help yourself. It's 'poor bull,' I know, but maybe it'll do to keep life in; and along the fleece thar's meat yet, and maybe my old hump ribs has picking on 'em."
>
> "You're a good old hos," answered La Bonté, "but this child ain't turned niggur yet." (*Life,* p. 127)

Frederick Manfred uses the passage to depict the delirium of Hugh Glass:

> Now, boy, I'll soon be under. Afore many hours. And, boy, if you don't raise meat pronto you'll be in the same fix I'm in. I've never et dead meat myself, Jim, and wouldn't ask you to do it neither. But meat fair killed is meat anyway. So, Jim, lad, put your knife in this old niggur's lights and help yourself. It's poor bull

> I am, I know, but maybe it'll do to keep life in ee.
> There should be some fleece on me that's meat yet.
> And maybe my old hump ribs has some pickin's on
> 'em in front. And there should be one roast left in my
> behind. Left side. Dig in lad, and drink man's blood.
> (*Lord Grizzly*, p. 213)

And in A. B. Guthrie's *The Big Sky*, Jim Deakins, wounded and near death, says to Boone Caudill:

> I ain't got long. When my mind's right I can see that
> much. I'll be under come tomorrow or next day. Ain't
> no use to say I'll make it. Ain't no use to try. Hear?
> Me and you never et dead meat, but meat fair-killed is
> meat to eat. There's a swaller or two on my old ribs.
> Take your knife, Boone. Get it out. I ain't got long,
> now, nohow. Goddam your old skin, you hear? Boone?
> (p. 308)

These examples show how far reaching the influence of this book has been over the years, and how often writers have turned to it for authentic details and episodes that give verisimilitude and richness to their work. (For a more complete discussion of this subject, see a forthcoming article by Richard H. Cracroft, " 'Half Froze for Mountain Doins': The Influence and Significance of George F. Ruxton's *Life in the Far West*.") The quality of Ruxton's imagination is sufficiently high to tempt other writers to borrow from him. He has not only rendered his subject with vigor and sensitivity, but in *Life* he has identified and gathered together many of the matters that our deepest concerns with the West have marked as significant.

More than merely a source book, *Life* stands as a prototype of the literature of the mountain man. The book has a consciously imaginative organization of materials which holds the disparate pieces in focus. It is not always the clear focus that we might hope for in a "great book," but for many other reasons the work has a right to its own claim as significant literature.

The account is replete with episodes of mountain life which are remarkably complete and satisfying set pieces. From the multi-chapter narratives such as the California horse-stealing expeditions to the page-long incidents around a campfire, these separate pieces are effective. In the first pages of the book, one of the mountain men responds to a query about seeing Indians:

> *Well,* we did. Some of em got their flints fixed this side of Pawnee Fork, and a heap of mule-meat went wolfing. Just by Little Arkansa we saw the first Injun. Me and young Somes was ahead for meat, and I had hobbled the old mule and was 'approaching' some goats when I see the critturs turn back their heads and jump right away for me. 'Hurraw, Dick!' I shouts, 'hyars brown-skin acomin,' and off I makes for the mule. The young greenhorn sees the goats runnin up to him, and not being up to Injun ways, blazes at the first and knocks him over. Jest then seven darned red heads top the bluff, and seven Pawnees come a-screechin upon us. I cuts the hobbles and jumps on the mule, and, when I looks back, there was Dick Somes ramming a ball down his gun like mad, and the Injuns flinging their arrows at him pretty smart, I tell you. 'Hurraw, Dick, mind your hair,' and I ups old Greaser and let one Injun 'have it,' as was going plum into the boy with his lance. *He* turned on his back handsome, and Dick gets the ball down at last, blazes away, and drops another. Then we charged on em, and they clears off like runnin cows; and I takes the hair off the heads of the two we made meat of; and I do b'lieve thar's some of them scalps on my old leggins yet. (*Life,* p. 12)

The pace of the passage is well sustained. Starting leisurely with generalizations about the episode to follow and with a careful fixing of place and purpose, the paragraph picks up narrative pace as explanations and transitional and introductory phrases and words give way to a minimum of precise, simple detail. From the past tense a careful shifting of verbs moves the narrative into a progressive present which gives the action both motion and immediacy. Moreover, the piece is a classic if miniature episode of initiation which recurs in such novels as *The Big Sky* and *Lord Grizzly*. Here is the familiar pair of mountaineers, the old-timer and the greenhorn, the latter as yet unlearned in the ways of Nature or Indians. The confrontation with the Western world is painful, but the pair survive by their own hardiness and skill, and the lesson is learned.

But the over-all outline of *Life* is also significant in its delineation of the career and character of La Bonté. To begin with, the image of the mountain man is larger than life, heroic in size and strength, as the fight at the Taos fandango makes plain:

> it happens that one of [the men], maddened by whisky and the green-eyed monster, suddenly seizes a fair one from the waist-encircling arm of a mountaineer, and pulls her from her partner. Wagh!—La Bonté—it is he —stands erect as a pillar for a moment, then raises his hand to his mouth, and gives a ringing war-whoop— jumps upon the rash *Peládo,* seizes him by the body as if he were a child, lifts him over his head, and dashes him with the force of a giant against the wall . . . . twenty Mexicans draw their knives and rush upon La Bonté, who stands his ground, and sweeps them down with his ponderous fist, one after another, as they throng around him. "Howgh-owgh-owgh-owgh-h!" the well-known war-whoop, bursts from the throats of his companions, and on they rush to the rescue. (pp. 188-89)

The cadences of the prose and the superiority of the mountain men have an epic quality that gives the passage a heroic dimension.

But La Bonté has more human qualities which make him more complex and interesting, even if less consistent as a literary figure. Following what was to become the type for mountain man life, La Bonté moves between the polar opposites of settlement and savage values. A flight from laws and domestic values begins the novel, followed by a sojourn dominated by the values of the wilderness, and at last by a return to civilization. But in moving La Bonté between these two antithetical poles of human values, Ruxton does not satisfactorily probe the contradictions between the civilized and wilderness life. Thus, after his initiation into mountain life, La Bonté seems at one point to have lost all traces of civilized values and to have become a true wilderness philosopher. As Ruxton describes him after his return to his ravaged camp: "La Bonté was a true philosopher. Notwithstanding that his house, his squaws, his peltries, were gone at one fell swoop, the loss scarcely disturbed his equanimity; and before the tobacco of his pipe was half smoked out, he had ceased to think of his misfortune. . . . He ate and smoked, and smoked and ate, and slept none the worse for his mishap . . ." (pp. 94-95). Any commitment to goods, to domestic life, to the past or the future, seems to have disappeared. But hardly a dozen pages later, Ruxton describes La Bonté in terms that suggest that the values usually associated with civilized existence are still an important part of the man: "If truth be told, La Bonté had his failings as a mountaineer, and —sin unpardonable in hunter law—still possessed, in holes and corners of his breast seldom explored by his inward eye, much of the leaven of kindly human nature . . . . Thus, in his various matrimonial episodes, he treated his dusky *sposas* with all the consideration the sex could possibly demand from hand of man" (p. 111).

If La Bonté discovers in his mountain wilderness a tough but nonetheless paradisaical existence, he nevertheless turns away from it at the slightest suggestion from Mary Brand, and, at the end of the book, turns his back on the wilderness to become a civilized husband.

Perhaps Ruxton felt compelled to create this ending by what he considered the conventions of the novel. But perhaps he felt, as well, a tension in his own bones that needed, if not resolution, at least understanding. If he was less than successful in realizing the potential in the pattern of La Bonté's existence, he came much closer when he surrounded La Bonté with a remarkable collection of mountain men who, taken together, become a revealing study in significant literary possibilities.

Old Bill Williams is a pure mountain man who, like a leitmotif, appears and disappears in the pages of the book. One of the first and oldest of mountain men, he ubiquitously emerges from bushes and "caches" to surprise his fellow fur trappers or to join them in an Indian battle. Crotchety and colorful, Williams stands out as an embodiment of the spirit of the mountains.

Life does not end with the romantic reunion of La Bonté and Mary Brand, but instead with the death of old Bill (a death, by the way, that has no basis in fact) : "burying as well as they were able, the body of the old mountaineer, the hunters next day left him in his lonely grave, in a spot so wild and remote, that it was doubtful whether even hungry wolves would discover and disinter his attenuated corpse" (p. 225).

If old Bill Williams is the spirit of the wilderness, Killbuck is the poet. In moments of contemplation, and with remarkable rhythms and imagery, he soliloquizes on the tensions that inform his life—the settlements vs. the mountains, nostalgia for times past vs. hope for a paradise to come:

> Thirty year have I been knocking about these mountains from Missoura's head as far sothe as the starving

> Gila. I've trapped a "heap," and many a hundred pack of beaver I've traded in my time, wagh! What has come of it, and whar's the dollars as ought to be in my possibles? Whar's the ind of this, I say? Is a man to be hunted by Injuns all his days? Many's the time I've said I'd strike for Taos, and trap a Squaw, for this child's getting old, and feels like wanting a woman's face about his lodge for the balance of his days; but when it comes to caching of the old traps, I've the smallest kind of heart, I have. . . . Beside, it goes against natur to leave bufler meat and feed on hog; and them white gals are too much like picturs, and a deal too "fofarraw" (fanfaron). No; darn the settlements, I say. (pp. 17-18)

If Killbuck's prose poem moves us to sympathy for his situation, it also touches our souls as we realize how closely our own dreams for a paradise parallel those of the old mountain man. Though Williams and Killbuck are two of the most significant figures in the book, they are by no means the only important ones. Kit Carson, Rube Herring, Dick Wooton, Markhead, Gonneville—each helps make a literary mosaic which, when viewed whole, depicts the values and complexities in the life of the mountain man that touched Ruxton and that continue to intrigue us.

Even though this world is a paradise of "boudins" and "fat fleece," a world of unparalleled freedom, it is also a place with a darker side—a world of violence and death. After feasting, the men are contented and sleep well; yet "not a night now passed but, when they lay down on their buffalo robes to sleep, they could not be confident that that sleep was not their last—knowing full well that savage men were hovering near, thirsting for their lives" (p. 63).

As in the case of Gonneville, death was often meaningless and unexpected. One of the bravest, he was shot, almost accidentally, by a stray bullet after the Indian battle was all but over, whereupon,

> With no other tools than their scalp-knives, the hunters dug a grave on the banks of the creek; and whilst some were engaged in this work, others sought the bodies of the Indians they had slain in the attack, and presently returned with three reeking scalps, the trophies of the fight. The body of the mountaineer was then wrapped in a buffalo robe, the scalps being placed on the dead man's breast, laid in the shallow grave, and quickly covered—without a word of prayer, or sigh of grief. . . .
>
> Trampling down the earth which filled the grave, they placed upon it a pile of heavy stones; and packing their mules once more, and taking a last look at their comrade's lonely resting-place, they turned their backs upon the stream, which has ever since been known as "Gonneville's Creek." (pp. 71-72)

The concrete detail of such passages recreates not only the feel of the experience but the meaning of the experience as well, for it heightens an awareness of the awful fragility of life.

Ruxton must have carried this awareness with him as he rode away from the mountains, thinking back on the experiences that he had felt in his muscles and in his mind. But it is one thing to have such an awareness and something else to develop a literary device that might deal with it adequately without violating the limited sophistication of the mountain man. That he found such a device is a mark of Ruxton's genius. For in his hands the mountain man vernacular becomes more than entertainment; it becomes a way of seeing, a way of coming to grips with the world. If the mountain man talks about "hind sights" and "dry powder," he may do so because these were his means of life; and if he has seen his own scribbling with a burnt stick "rubbed out," the experience gives him a means of dealing with death even if he does not understand it.

For this reason, Black Harris's narrative of the "putrefied forest" becomes a classic expression of the mountain man. The language is not only epic and expansive, but the tale is also real in its allusions and metaphors. If the spirit of the narrative is proud and comprehensive, the tale itself is of a world that is disturbing, a world where natural law no longer holds, a world in which reality and unreality are so blended as to seem, for a time at least, indistinguishable:

> Black Harris come in from Laramie; he'd been trapping three year an' more on Platte and the 'other side'; and, when he got into Liberty, he fixed himself right off like a Saint Louiy dandy. Well, he sat to dinner one day in the tavern, and a lady says to him:
>
> "Well, Mister Harris, I hear you're a great travler."
>
> "Travler, marm,'" says Black Harris, "this niggur's no travler; I ar' a trapper, marm, a mountain-man, wagh!"
>
> "Well, Mister Harris, trappers are great travlers, and you goes over a sight of ground in your perishinations, I'll be bound to say."
>
> "A sight, marm, this coon's gone over, if that's the way your 'stick floats.' I've trapped beaver on Platte and Arkansa, and away up on Missoura and Yaller Stone; I've trapped on Columbia, on Lewis Fork, and Green River; I've trapped, marm, on Grand River and the Heely (Gila). I've fout the 'Blackfoot' (and d--d bad Injuns they are); I've 'raised the hair' of more *than one* Apach, and made a Rapaho 'come' afore now; I've trapped in heav'n, in airth, and h--, and scalp my old head, marm, but I've seen a putrefied forest."
>
> "La, Mister Harris, a what?"

"A putrefied forest, marm, as sure as my rifle's got hindsights, and *she* shoots center. I was out on the Black Hills, Bill Sublette knows the time—the year it rained fire—and everybody knows when that was. If thar wasn't cold doin's about that time, this child wouldn't say so. The snow was about fifty foot deep, and the buffler lay dead on the ground like bees after a beein'; not whar we was tho', for *thar* was no bufler, and no meat, and me and my band had been livin' on our moccasins (leastwise the parflesh), for six weeks; and poor doin's that feedin' is, marm, as you'll never know. One day we crossed a 'canon' and over a 'divide,' and got into a periara, whar was green grass, and green trees, and green leaves on the trees, and birds singing in the green leaves, and this in Febrary, wagh! Our animals was like to die when they see the green grass, and we all sung out 'hurraw for summer doin's.'

" 'Hyar goes for meat,' says I, and I jest ups old Ginger at one of them singing birds, and down come the crittur elegant; its darned head spinning away from the body, but never stops singing, and when I takes up the meat, I finds it stone, wagh!

"Hyar's damp powder and no fire to dry it," I says quite skeared.

" 'Fire be dogged,' says old Rube. 'Hyar's a hos as'll make fire come'; and with that he takes his axe and lets drive at a cottonwood. Schr-u-k—goes the axe agin the tree, and out comes a bit of the blade as big as my hand. We looks at the animals, and thar they stood shaking over the grass, which I'm dog-gone if it wasn't stone, too. Young Sublette comes up, and he'd been clerking down to the fort on Platte, so he know'd something. He looks and looks, and scrapes the tree with his butcher knife, and snaps the grass like pipe stems and breaks the leaves a-snappin' like Californy shells.

" 'What's all this, boy?' I asks.

" 'Putrefactions,' says he, looking smart, 'putrefactions, or I'm a niggur.' "

"La, Mister Harris," says the lady; "putrefactions, why, did the leaves, and the trees, and the grass smell badly?"

"Smell badly, marm," says Black Harris, "would a skunk stink if he was froze to stone?" (pp. 7-9)

The Black Harris anecdote amuses and entertains, but it also presents the *donnée* of early Western experience. As Richard Cracroft says in a recent manuscript: "He [Ruxton] has asked, or at least tacitly raised, many of the literary questions which would move later novelists to try again to find meaning in the buffalo hunts, the stalking, the slaughtering, the scalping, the cannibalism; to find in the lonely hunts under vast skies, the solitary camps, the sudden deaths some wider philosophical meaning in that reckless breed of men—and in that reckless breed called mankind" ("Half Froze for Mountain Doins").

More than civilized man, whose suns rise and set at the flick of a switch, the mountain man realized his own close dependence upon nature, upon the steady progress of seasons, the flow of water, the birth and death of game. If his own dependence led him to raise questions about the nature of Nature, he can hardly be blamed. There was, after all, always the darkness beyond the fire. Confronted daily with forces he could not control, he felt he could not comprehend them either, and so he chose, if subconsciously, to deal with that world through the oblique tropes of his speech. In seeing this, Ruxton became not only the first, but also one of the most significant novelists of the fur trade.

Selected Bibliography

This bibliography contains only those items which might be considered essential to an understanding of Ruxton. For a more complete list including manuscripts, reviews, etc., see the material in Storm, *A Catalogue of The Everett D. Graff Collection*, and Buell's bibliography in the Rio Grande Press reprint of the first edition of *Adventures in Mexico and the Rocky Mountains*.

PRIMARY SOURCES

Porter, Clyde, and Mae Reed Porter, collectors; and LeRoy Hafen, editor. *Ruxton of the Rockies*. Norman: University of Oklahoma Press, 1950.

Ruxton, George [Augustus] F[rederick]. *Adventures in Mexico and the Rocky Mountains*. London: John Murray, 1847.

———, Esq. *Adventures in Mexico and the Rocky Mountains*. 1847. Reprint. Glorieta, New Mexico: The Rio Grande Press, 1973.

———. *Life in the Far West*. Edinburgh: William Blackwood and Sons, 1849.

———. *Life in the Far West*. 1849. Reprint of the first edition with added sub-title "Among the Indians and the Mountain Men, 1846-47." Glorieta, New Mexico: The Rio Grande Press, 1972.

———. *Life in the Far West*. Edited by LeRoy R. Hafen. Norman: University of Oklahoma Press, 1951.

———, Lieutenant. "Notes on the South-west Coast of Africa." *Nautical Magazine and Naval Chronicle,* January 1846.

———. *The Oregon Question*. London: John Ollivier, 1846.

———. "Sketches of the Mexican War." *Fraser's Magazine,* 38 (July 1848), 97-102.

SECONDARY SOURCES

Abert, Lieut. James W. *Western America in 1846-47: The Original travel diary of Lieutenant J. W. Abert who mapped New Mexico for the United States Army.* Ed. John Galvin. San Francisco: John Howell-Books, 1966.

Cracroft, Richard H. *"The Big Sky*: A. B. Guthrie's Use of Historical Sources." *Western American Literature,* 6 (Fall 1971), 163-76. See also his forthcoming article " 'Half Froze for Mountain Doins': The Influence and Significance of George F. Ruxton's *Life in the Far West."*

Garrard, Lewis H[ector]. *Wah-To-Yah and the Taos Trail.* The Western Frontier Library. Norman: University of Oklahoma Press, 1955.

Grinnell, George Bird. *Beyond the Old Frontier: Adventures of Indian-fighters, hunters, and fur-traders.* New York: Scribner's, 1913.

"The Late George Frederick Ruxton." *Blackwood's Edinburgh Magazine,* 64 (November 1848), 591-94.

Munro, J. "Ruxton of the Rocky Mountains." *Good Words,* 34 (August 1893), 547-51.

Poulsen, Richard L. "Black George, Black Harris, and the Mountain Man Vernacular." *Rendezvous,* 8 (Summer 1973), 15-23.

Schaefer, Jack [Warner]. *Heroes Without Glory: some good men of the Old West.* Boston: Houghton Mifflin Company (Riverside Press, Cambridge), 1965.

Storm, Colton. *A Catalogue of the Everett D. Graff Collection of Western Americana.* Chicago: The University of Chicago Press, 1968.

Sutherland, Bruce. "George Frederick Ruxton in North America." *Southwest Review,* 30 (Autumn 1944), 86-91.

Voelker, Frederic E. "Ruxton of the Rocky Mountains." *Missouri Historical Bulletin,* 5 (January 1949), 79-90.

Walker, Don D. "The Mountain Man as Literary Hero." *Western American Literature,* 1 (Spring 1966), 15-25. See also his forthcoming literary history of the fur trade.

WESTERN WRITERS SERIES

General Editors: Wayne Chatterton and James H. Maguire
Boise State University

This continuing series, primarily regional in nature, provides brief but authoritative introductions to the lives and works of authors who have written significant literature about the American West. These attractive, uniform pamphlets, none of them longer than fifty pages, will be useful to the general reader as well as to high school and college students.

Currently Available:

1. V... THE FRONTIER AND REGIONAL WORKS by Wayne Chatterton
2. MARY HALLOCK FOOTE by James H. Maguire
3. JOHN MUIR by Thomas J. Lyon
4. WALLACE STEGNER by Merrill and Lorene Lewis
5. BRET HARTE by Patrick Morrow.
6. THOMAS HORNSBY FERRIL by A. Thomas Trusky
7. OWEN WISTER by Richard Etulain
8. WALTER VAN TILBUR... L. L. Lee
9. ... MOMADAY by M... tha Scott Trimble
10. PLAINS INDIAN AUTOBIOGRAPHIES by Lynne Woods O'Brien

Available Fall 1974:

11. H. L. DAVIS by Robert B...
12. KEN KESEY by Bruce Carr...
13. FREDERICK MANFRED... Joseph M. Flora
14. WASHINGTON IRVING: THE WESTERN WORKS by Richard Cracroft
15. GEORGE FREDERICK RUXTON by Neal Lambert

IN PREPARATION

GERTRUDE ATHERTON by Merrill Lewis; J. ROSS BROWNE by Thomas H. Pau... GEORGE CATLIN by Joseph R. Millichap; EDWIN CORLE by William Pilkington; HAMLIN GARLAND by Robert F. Gish; ZANE GREY by Ann Ronald; E. W. HOWE by Ma... Bucco; DOROTHY JOHNSON by Ernest L. Bulow; ROBINSON JEFFERS by Robert Brophy; JACK KEROUAC by Harry Russell Huebel; JOSEPH WOOD KRUTCH by... Golden Taylor; ALFRED HENRY LEWIS by Abe C. Ravitz; FREDERIC REMINGTON... Fred Erisman; JACK SCHAEFER by Gerald Haslam; STEWART EDWARD WHITE... Judy Alter.

FORTHCOMING TITLES

Edward Abbey, Paul Bailey, Charles Wolcott Balestier, Raymond Barrio, Don Berry, Ar... Binns, Robert Bly, Richard Brautigan, Struthers Burt, Robert Cantwell, Benjamin Ca... Vine Deloria, Jr., Bernard DeVoto, Charles Alexander Eastman, Lawrence Ferlingh... Josiah Gregg, William Inge, Helen Hunt Jackson, Will James, Clarence King, Frank... Linderman, Mabel Dodge Luhan, Edwin Markham, Joaquin Miller, John R. Milton, Ho... Willsie Morrow, John G. Neihardt, Bill Nye, Martha Ostenso, Edward Ricketts, Elizab... Robins, Rocky Mountain Reminiscences, Will Rogers, Theodore Roosevelt, Charles Russ... Mari Sandoz, William Saroyan, Gary Snyder, Virginia Sorensen, Jean Stafford, Willi... Stafford, James Stevens, George R. Stewart, Alan Swallow, Stanley Vestal, David Wago... Paul I. Wellman, Thames Ross Williamson, Yvor Winters, Sophus K. Winther, Cha... Erskine Scott Wood.

EACH PAMPHLET $1.50

DEPARTMENT OF ENGLISH
BOISE STATE UNIVERSITY
BOISE, IDAHO 83725